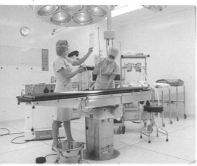

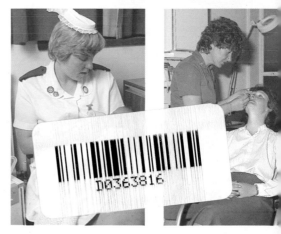

If ever you have visited or been admitted to a hospital you will have seen the many dedicated men and women who are nurses, at work. There are also many other kinds of nurses working in the community. This book, written in simple language for young children and illustrated with full colour photographs, specially taken for the book, describes the working lives of nurses and takes children behind the scenes.

Acknowledgments
The author and publishers would like to thank the following for their help, advice and co-operation during the preparation of this book: the staff and patients at Leicester Royal Infirmary; the staff and students at the Charles Freer School of Nursing, Leicester; the United Kingdom Central Council for Nursing Midwifery and Health Visiting; Leicestershire Ambulance Service; Westcotes Health Centre, Leicester; Wyman, Hammond and Padmore – Dental Surgeons, Loughborough; Fisons PLC, Loughborough; Adam and Mrs R. M. Perkins; and Sally and Mr and Mrs E. Jolley. The photographs on page 51 are by kind permission of the Department of Clinical Photography, Royal Naval Hospital, Haslar.

First Edition

© LADYBIRD BOOKS LTD MCMLXXXIII

People who help us

THE NURSE

written by ANN MARCELLI
photographs by TIM CLARK

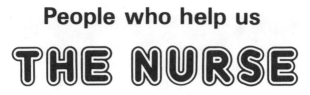

Ladybird Books Loughborough

Two nurses go off duty from their work at a large city hospital

If ever you have had a bad accident, or been very ill, or needed an operation, you will have been taken to a hospital.

There you will have been looked after by doctors and others and many men and women who are *nurses.*

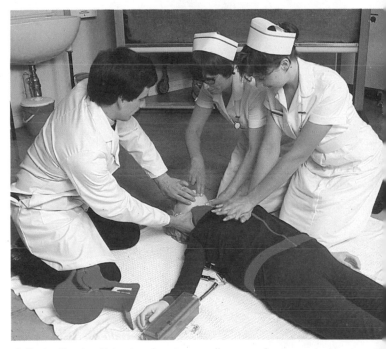

A Senior Nursing Tutor teaches two pupil nurses about resuscitation. They practise this using a dummy

There are over 360,000 nurses working in the National Health Service. Some of these nurses are *training*. They are called *student nurses* or *pupil nurses*.

A district nurse visits a patient's home

Not all nurses work in hospitals. There are *community* or *district nurses* and *health visitors* who work alongside the family doctor. They work in health centres or clinics and visit patients at home.

Some nurses care for people who are mentally ill, or people who are handicapped. Other nurses look after old people.

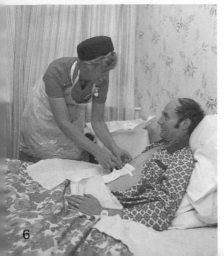

This man has recently had an operation. The nurse changes his dressing and checks that he is continuing to get better

Dentists have their own nurses called *dental nurses*. They help the dentist when you go for a filling or other treatment to your teeth. They are trained by the dentist.

A dental nurse helps a dentist with his patient

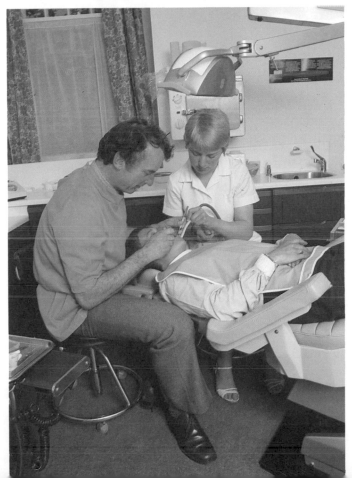

One of the most famous of all nurses was Florence Nightingale. She was known as 'the lady with the lamp' and she worked to help wounded soldiers in the Crimean War over 100 years ago. She started the idea of nursing as we know it today.

Florence Nightingale 1820-1910

Many people who go to a hospital have to go there quickly because of an accident or an emergency where they have been taken ill very suddenly.

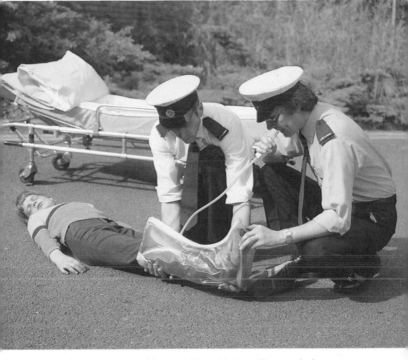

Adam has had an accident and hurt his leg. Two ambulance men put his leg in an inflatable splint to prevent further injury and pain

If these patients are too sick to get to the hospital themselves they will be taken in an *ambulance*.

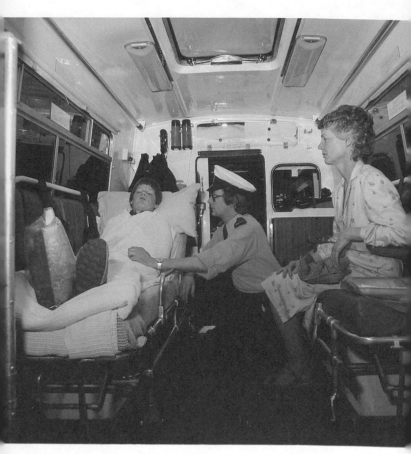

Adam is taken to hospital in an ambulance. His mother goes with him. The ambulance man makes sure that he is comfortable

Ambulance drivers are specially trained to help sick or injured people in an emergency, until they reach the hospital.

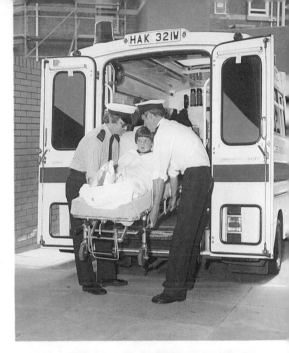

At the hospital, Adam is carefully lifted out of the ambulance and wheeled into the Accident and Emergency Department

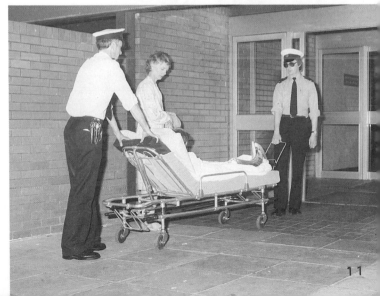

All these *patients* go to the *Casualty* or *Accident and Emergency Department* of the hospital.

Adam's mother tells reception his name, age and address and what has happened. This information is written on a card

Here the doctors will *examine* them and the nurses will give them *treatment*.

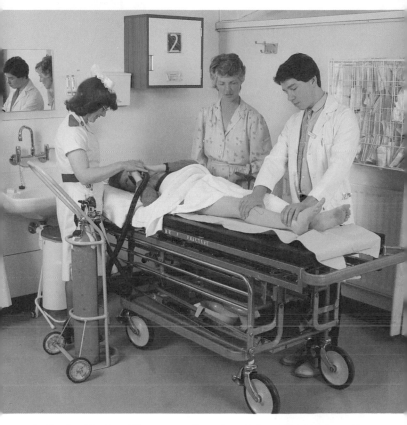

In the Accident and Emergency Department the splint is taken off and a doctor examines Adam's leg. His leg hurts so a nurse helps to make him more comfortable. His mother goes with Adam

A patient may need *stitches* or a *dressing* for a bad cut.

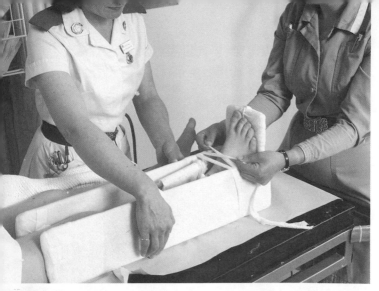

The doctor would like to see an X-ray photograph of the leg. The nurses gently put Adam's leg into a box splint *so that it cannot move and become more painful while the X-ray is being taken*

If you have had a bad fall at home or at school the doctor may send you to the *X-ray department*. A nurse will go with you.

Left: *The radiographer loads the special X-ray film*

Right: *The film is placed under the leg and the camera is positioned to take the photograph*

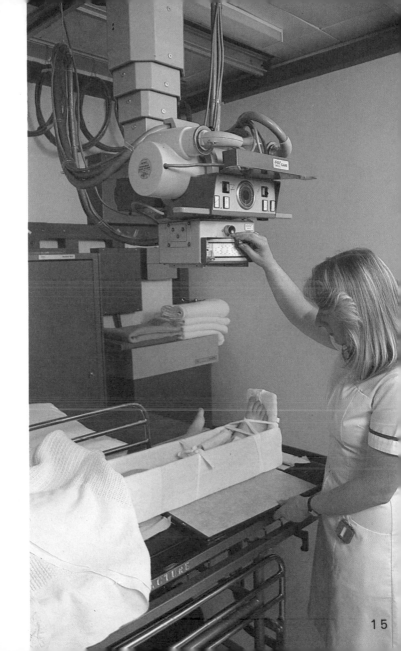

An X-ray photograph does not hurt but it will show the doctor, very quickly, whether a bone has been broken.

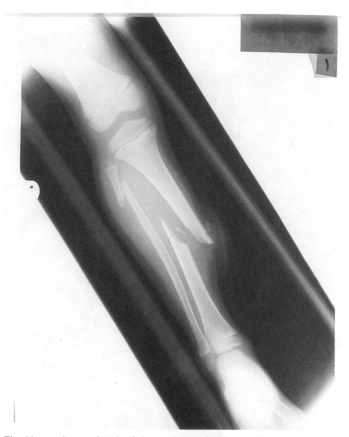

The X-ray shows that both bones in the leg below the knee have been broken.
The larger bone is the tibia *and the smaller bone is the* fibula

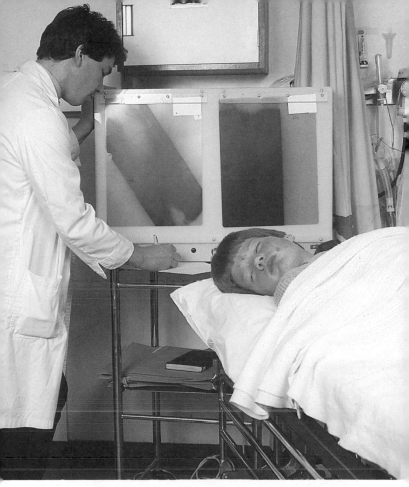

The doctor checks the X-ray and writes some comments on Adam's card. This will tell the nurses what treatment to give Adam

If it has, the nurse will help to put the arm, leg, or other part of the body, in plaster before you go home.

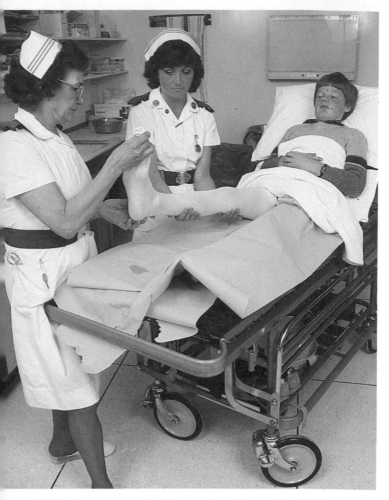

Broken bones are set in plaster to keep them still while they grow together again.

In the plaster room the nurses first cover Adam's injured leg with a soft stocking. Over the stocking they wrap some thicker, soft wadding

Finally, plaster of paris bandages are dipped in water, unwound round and round the leg and smoothed down. The plaster is dry in about an hour but it takes a day to become really hard

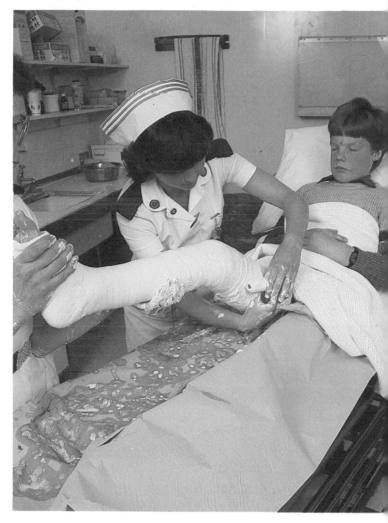

Patients who are very ill or badly injured will stay at the hospital and be taken to a *ward* by a nurse. Many people know that they have to go into hospital for treatment or an operation.

Sally has come into hospital for an operation. She and her father report to the main reception desk where a form is filled in for them to take up to the ward

When there is a bed for them, these people will come to the hospital ward from home.

A *ward assistant* will write down the names, ages, addresses and other details of all patients coming into the ward.

The ward assistant admits Sally to one of the children's wards

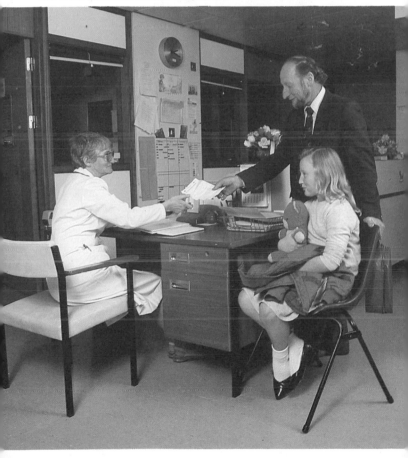

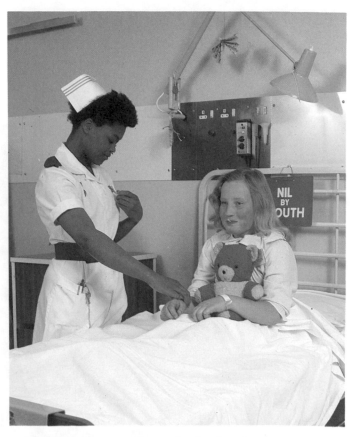

When the patient is in bed a nurse
will come and take his or her
temperature and *pulse*.
Sometimes there are other tests for the
nurse to do such as weighing patients
or taking their *blood pressure*.

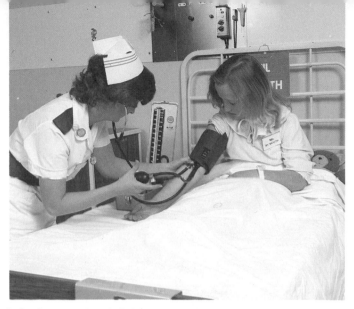

Left: *A nurse takes Sally's temperature and pulse*
Above: *Another nurse takes her blood pressure*

The nurse writes the results of all these tests on a chart which usually hangs at the foot of the patient's bed.

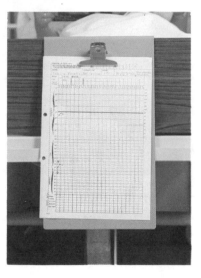

The sign on the bed, NIL BY MOUTH, tells other nurses and ward staff that Sally must have nothing to eat or drink before her operation

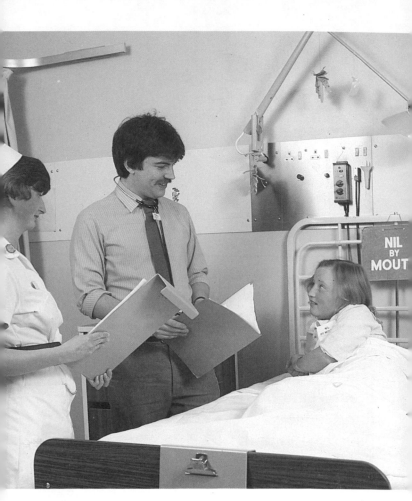

Soon a hospital doctor will come and
see each patient in the ward and tell
the nurse in charge what *medicine* or
treatment to give to each person.

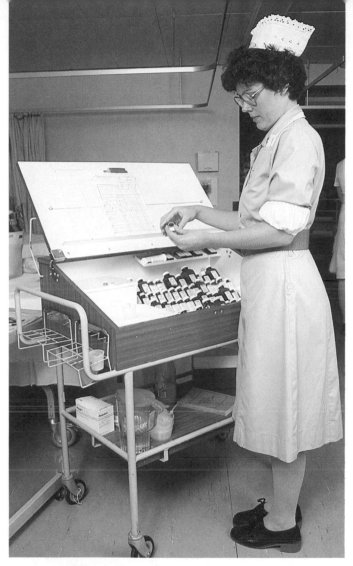

A doctor tells the ward sister what medicine to give to patients. It is stored in a lockable trolley and the correct amount is given out each day

Day and night there are nurses on duty on the wards to look after the patients. In charge of the wards are *Ward Sisters* or *Charge Nurses*.

Above: *A student nurse training for the general register*

Below: *The uniform worn by Enrolled Nurses in this hospital*

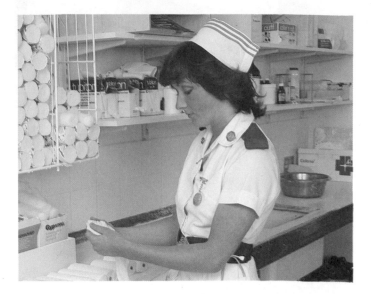

There are other experienced nursing officers in charge of these nurses and they work hard in the running of the hospital.

A Ward Sister   *A Charge Nurse*

Nurses wear different types and colours of uniforms in different hospitals but the Ward Sister usually has a plain dress in one colour and sometimes a frilly hat. The Charge Nurse is a *male nurse* and he wears a short white coat with coloured epaulettes on his shoulders.

All those who want to be nurses study hard and have to pass exams, as well as working on the wards with patients, before they are *qualified*.

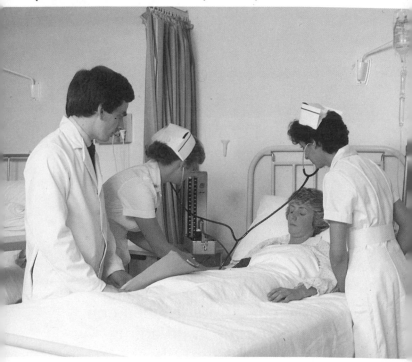

Two pupil nurses learn to take a patient's blood pressure. The special double-stethoscope enables them both to hear what each other is doing

There are different kinds of nurses: Enrolled Nurses (E.N.) train for two years; Registered General Nurses (R.G.N.)

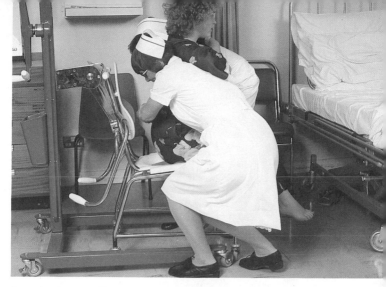

Learning how to lift a patient correctly

train for three years. There are many nurses who qualified some time ago called S.R.N. which means State Registered Nurse and this is the same as R.G.N.

Studying in the School of Nursing library

When they have passed their exams, nurses can go on to study different types of nursing.

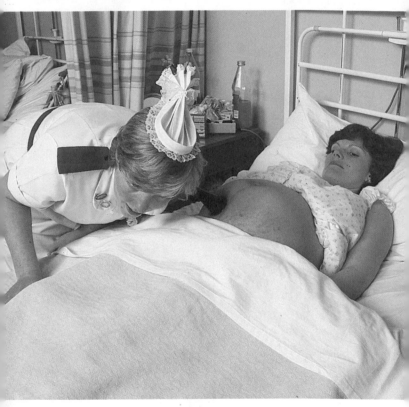

A midwife listens to the heartbeat of an unborn baby

Some nurses may train to be *midwives*. They look after women who are having babies and work in the

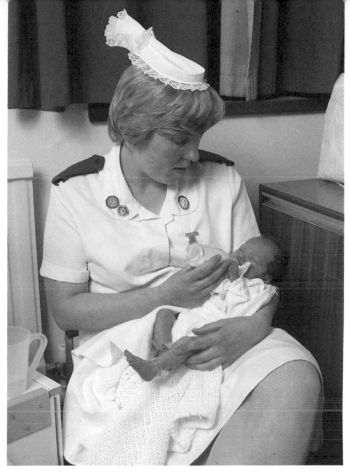
Nurses often help to feed the new-born babies. This little girl is only eight days old

maternity ward in a hospital or in the mothers' homes. People can become midwives without training to be general nurses first.

Many people choose to train to be special kinds of nurses from the beginning. For example, *psychiatric nursing* is working with those who are mentally ill. *Pediatric nurses* work in children's wards.

A Sister helps to give lunch to a patient

Registered Nurses and other special types of nurses can often become Ward Sisters or Charge Nurses after a few years. Other staff you may meet on a ward are called *nursing auxiliaries*. There are over 120,000 of these, and they learn how to help the patients and give food and drinks to people. They are a great help to the nurses.

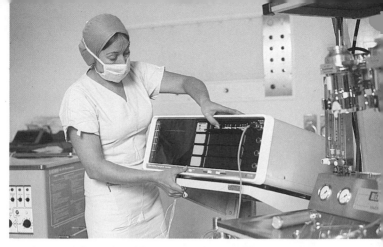

An electrocardiograph (ECG). This machine monitors a patient's heartbeat

Larger hospitals have separate wards for different types of illnesses. These days nurses need to learn to use many different kinds of machines and equipment to help their patients.

A nurse adjusts a drip to give blood to this patient

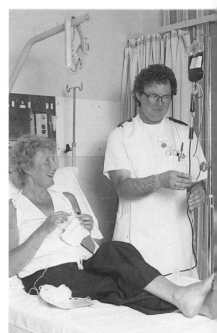

Within a large ward there are separate smaller wards for men and women.

A student nurse helps the Sister on a medical ward to give medicine to the patients

A *medical ward* is one where patients are given medicine or other treatment to make them well.

A *surgical ward* is one for those people who need an operation. When it is an emergency, patients go straight to the operating theatre.

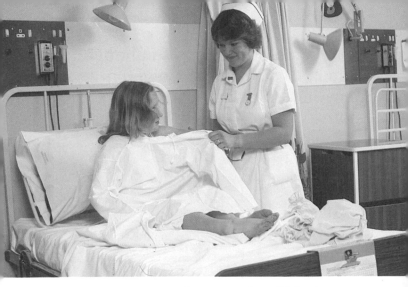

If not, a nurse on the ward will help
to get a patient ready for an operation.

Above and below: *Sally wears a special gown and hat to go for
her operation*

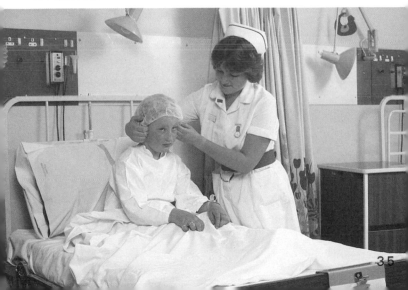

The nurse often gives the patient an injection or a tablet to make him or her sleepy before going to the *operating theatre*.

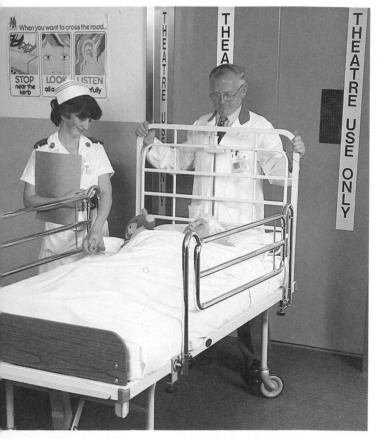

A porter wheels Sally, in her bed to the operating theatre. A nurse goes with her

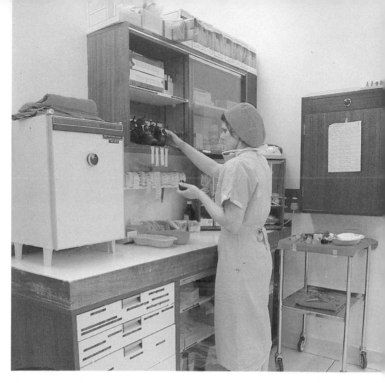

In the anaesthetic room

The patient is then looked after by specially trained people. Some nurses are specially trained to help the *surgeons*, who do the operations. In the room just outside the operating theatre the *anaesthetist* will put the patient to sleep straightaway. When the patient next wakes up, the operation is all over.

The operating theatre

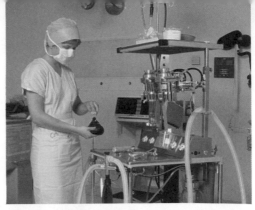

Preparing the apparatus for giving anaesthetic to a patient during an operation

Nurses working in the operating theatre have to scrub their hands and arms very thoroughly with a strong antiseptic soap.

All nurses and other staff working in the operating theatre wear special shoes, uniform and hats.

They must all wear masks so that they don't breathe germs over anything to be used during an operation

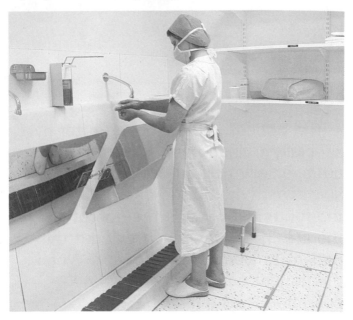

After careful washing, the nurse does not touch anything that is not sterile (germ free). Her theatre gown is taken from a sealed package and another nurse helps her to dress. She then puts on very thin rubber gloves taken from another sterile pack

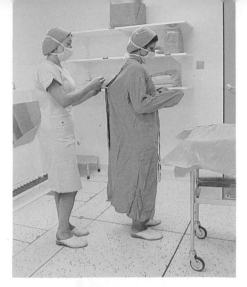

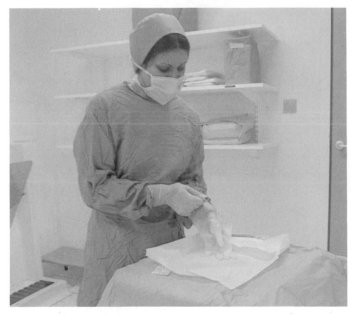

This nurse then unpacks and lays out all the instruments for the surgeon. Again, these are taken from a sterile package

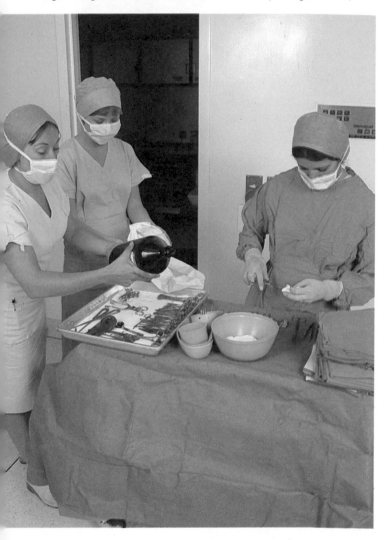

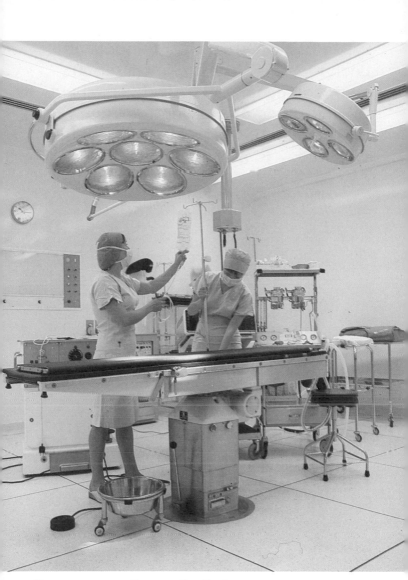

The nurses prepare the operating theatre

A nurse will then take the patient back to the ward. Straight after an operation people often feel very ill but the nurses do everything they can to make the patients feel better and get well, ready to go home.

Sally is sleeping after her operation.
A nurse makes sure she is comfortable

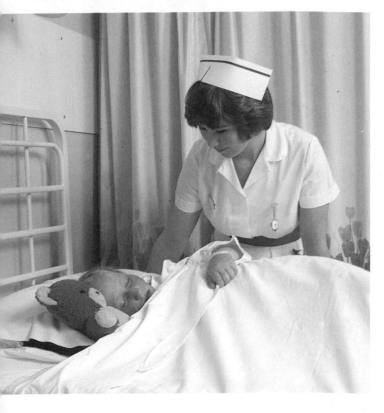

A Night Sister on duty

Even at night nurses are on duty to
care for the patients. Sometimes a
patient has to come into hospital
during the night. A Night Sister or
Charge Nurse or a *Staff Nurse* is in
charge of the ward at night. He or she
will write down anything which
happens during the night to tell the day
nurses in the morning. Nurses take it in
turns to work in the day or at night.

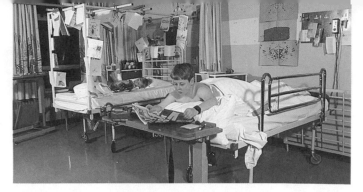

Some hospital wards are especially for children. In a few places there are whole hospitals just for children.

Above and below: *Children's wards are very bright, happy places*

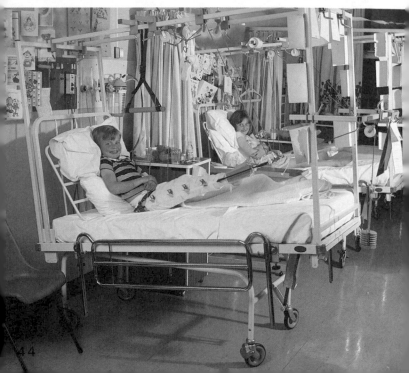

Parents can usually visit their children at any time of the day, or even stay overnight in a room near the ward.

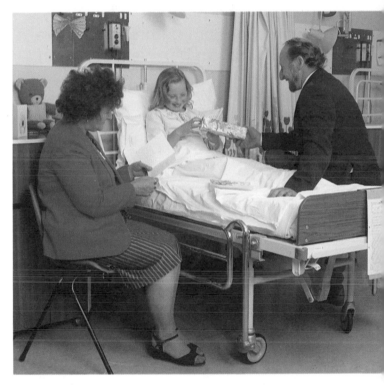

Mothers and fathers do a lot to help the busy nurses. They feed, dress, bath and play with their children while they are in hospital.

If children are in hospital for a long time they will go to a special school which is inside the hospital. Children who must stay in bed are visited on the ward by the teacher. When they have any spare time, nurses who are helping children to get well will often

A nursery nurse plays a game with Sally while she waits for her appointment

read stories or play games with them. There are also trained *nursery nurses* to help with this.

When people are well again they go home. Sometimes patients have to come back to visit the hospital after a few weeks.

Sally is measured

The doctors may want to check that the treatment or operation has worked and that the patient is quite better.

She is also weighed. This helps the doctor to know that she is getting better after her operation

People who have had broken bones need to come back to have the plaster cast taken off.

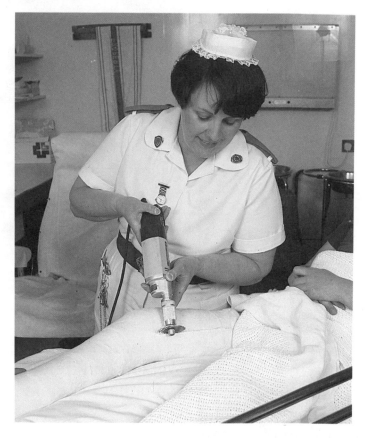

The nurse uses a special circular saw to cut off Adam's plaster. It vibrates backwards and forwards very quickly to cut through the hard plaster but it will not cut soft bandage or a patient's skin. This machine makes a lot of noise but it will not hurt the patient

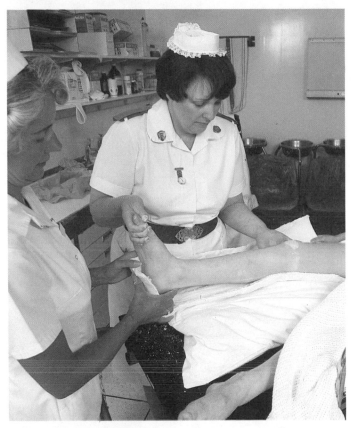

When the plaster is removed the nurses lift Adam's healed and mended leg out of the cast. It feels strange at first but he can now walk on it again and it will soon feel completely better

All these people go to the *Out-patients Department*. This is a very busy place and nurses work hard to help the doctors.

Nurses in hospitals, those working in towns and villages with patients at home, nurses in schools or factories

A factory nurse checks that all the health and safety rules are being observed

A factory nurse removes something from an employee's eye

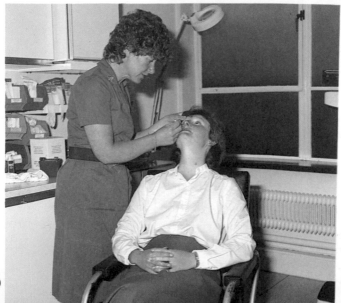

and those in the Army, Navy or Air Force all work very hard. Whatever kinds of nurses they are, all of them are proud of their work. But the best part of their job is seeing their patients get well again!

A member of the Queen Alexandra's Royal Naval Nursing Service (QARNNS)
A Naval nurse and medical assistant at a Royal Naval Air Station

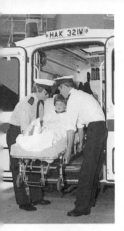

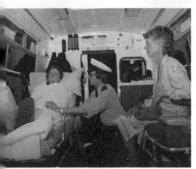
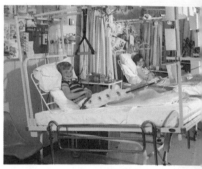